Mission Ziffoid

Michael Rosen
Illustrated by Arthur Robins

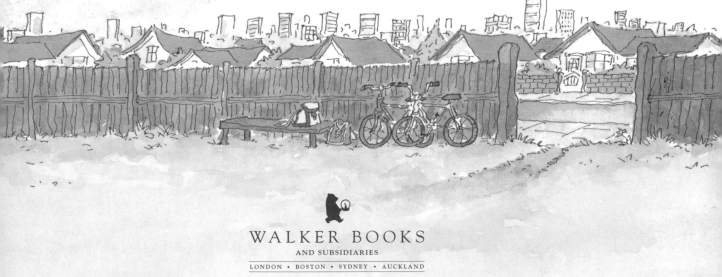

WALKER BOOKS
AND SUBSIDIARIES
LONDON · BOSTON · SYDNEY · AUCKLAND

"Guess what? My brother's got a spaceship
with four mega-blast booster rockets."

Little Funnies

Little Funnies is a delightful collection of picture books made to put a giggle into storytime.

There are funny stories about a laughing lobster, a daring mouse, a teeny tiny woman, and lots more colourful characters!

Perfect for sharing, these rib-tickling tales will have your little ones coming back for more!

TEE HEE!

HA HA!

For Lee – A. R.

"Wow! That's good."

"No, that's bad. On the
way to Mars, the spaceship
exploded into a million bits."

"Gosh! That's bad."

"No, he escaped
in his ejector seat."

"That's good."

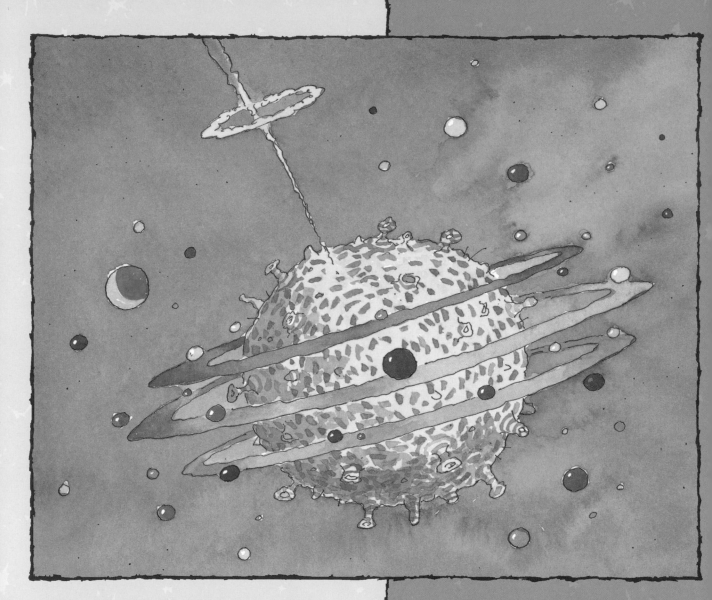

"No! That's bad. He crash-landed on Ziffoid, a weird planet zillions of miles away."

"Wow! That's bad."

"No, he landed on some lovely soft stuff and wasn't hurt at all."

"That's good."

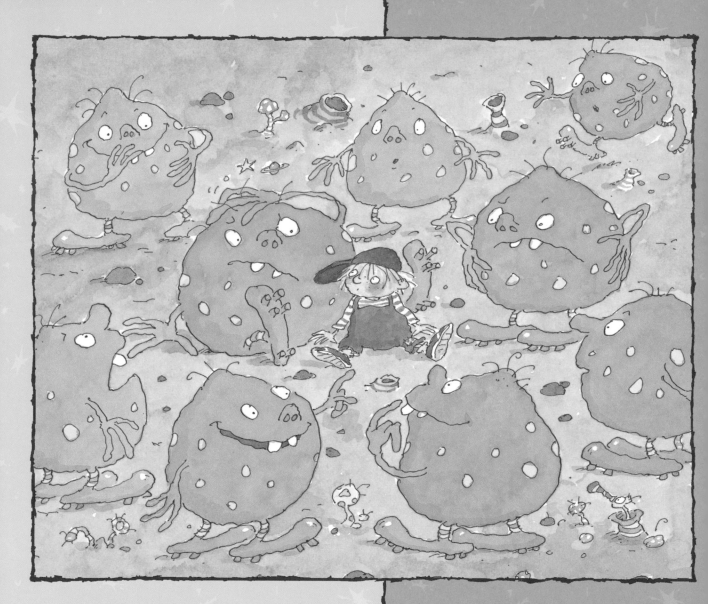

"No! That's bad.
The lovely soft stuff
was a family of aliens."

"Ugh! That's bad."

"Oh no, that's good. The aliens thought he'd come to play football with them."

"That's good."

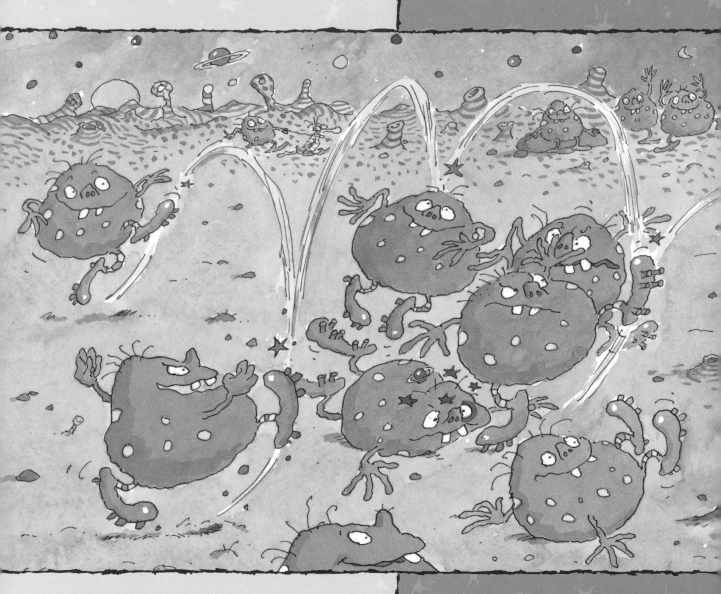

"No! That's bad.
My brother was the ball."

"Yikes! That *is* bad."

"No! That's good...

They kicked him into
their spaceship."

"Is that good?"

"No, that's bad. The aliens followed him inside."

"Oh, that's bad."

"No, that's good.
They said he could use
their spaceship to fly home."

"That *is* good."

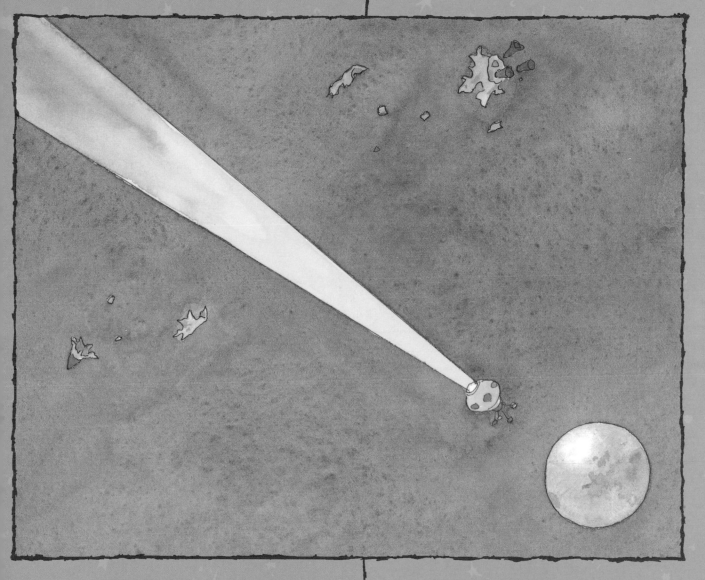

"No, no, no! That is *bad*."   **"Why?"**

"Because...
     Guess what?

The aliens came with him!”

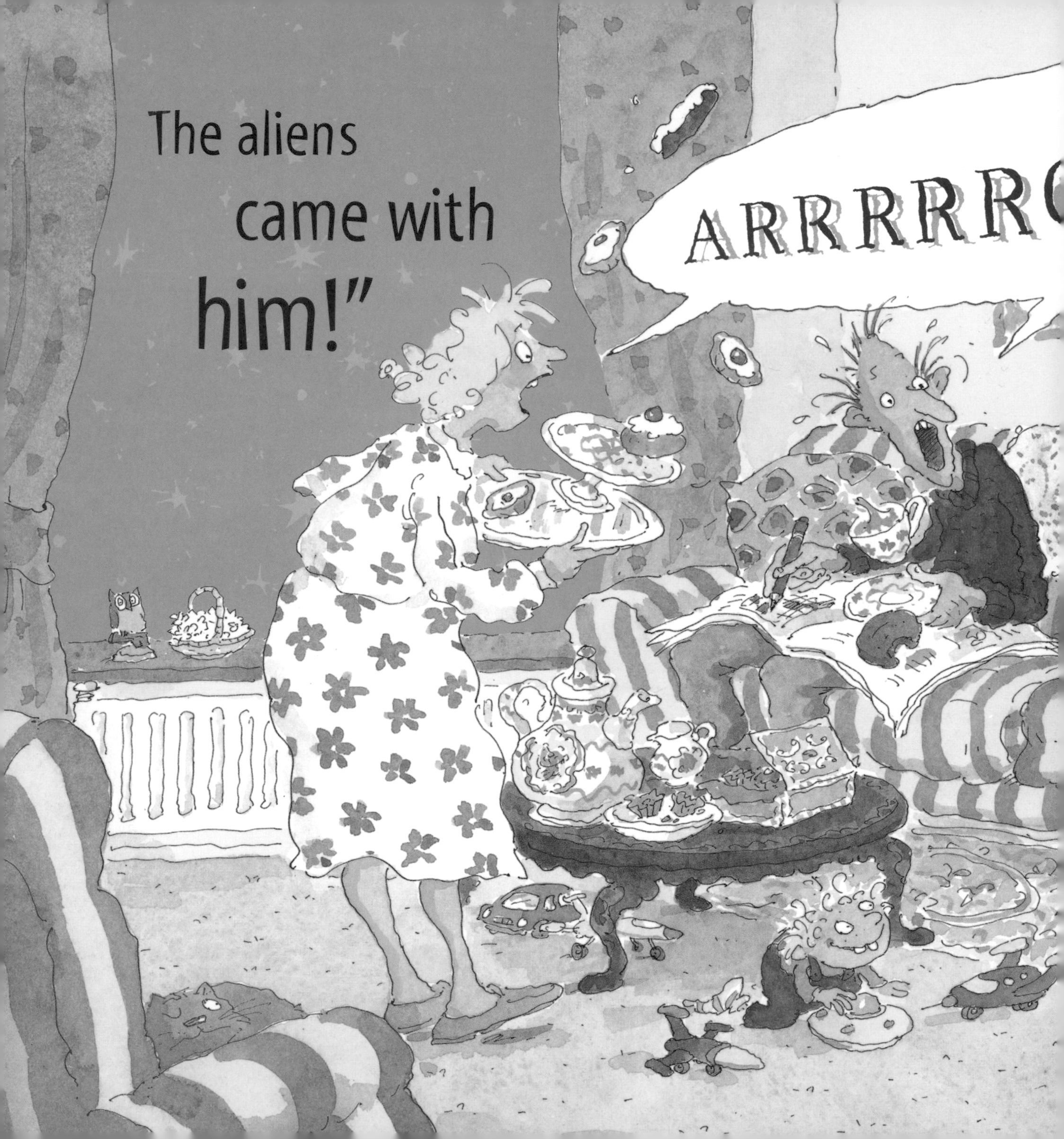

First published 1999 by Walker Books Ltd, 87 Vauxhall Walk, London SE11 5HJ

This edition published 2007

2 4 6 8 10 9 7 5 3 1

Text © 1999 Michael Rosen   Illustrations © 1999 Arthur Robins

The moral rights of the author/illustrator have been asserted.

This book has been typeset in Myriad Tilt.

Printed in China

British Library Cataloguing in Publication Data:
a catalogue record for this book is is available from the British Library.

ISBN 978-1-4063-0788-7

www.walkerbooks.co.uk